Liam Knows What To Do When Kids Act Snitty

Coping When Friends are Tactless

Jane Whelen Banks

Jessica Kingsley Publishers
London and Philadelphia

First published in 2009
by Jessica Kingsley Publishers
116 Pentonville Road
London N1 9JB, UK
and
400 Market Street, Suite 400
Philadelphia, PA 19106, USA

www.jkp.com

Library of Congress Cataloging in Publication Data
Banks, Jane Whelen.
 Liam knows what to do when kids act snitty : coping when friends are tactless / Jane Whelen Banks.
  p. cm.
 ISBN 978-1-84310-902-0 (pb : alk. paper)
 1. Courtesy--Juvenile literature. 2. Friendship--Juvenile literature. 3. Interpersonal relations--Juvenile literature. 4. Conduct
of life--Juvenile literature. I. Title.
 BJ1533.C9B36 2009
 155.4'18--dc22
                                        2008017768

British Library Cataloguing in Publication Data
A CIP catalogue record for this book is available from the British Library

ISBN 978 1 84310 902 0

Printed and bound in China by
Reliance Printing Co, Ltd.

Dedication

To Sarah: Thank you for being a friend, for being playful and imaginative, for being fair, and especially for being so utterly honest.

Acknowledgment

I would like to acknowledge Stephanie Loo from the Asperger's Association of New England for her ongoing encouragement, her heartening emails, her professional perspective, and for taking the time to listen.

Human social behavior is sophisticated and complex. While we can teach our preschoolers the simple action–reaction emotions of happy, sad, fear, and anger, how do we approach less predictable social feedback such as sarcasm, indifference, and spitefulness, to name a few? Desirable or not, these are among the many responses our children will face in their lifetime. While predicting and understanding them may be difficult, if not impossible, our children must still learn to cope with them.

In **Liam Knows What To Do When Kids Act Snitty**, Liam eagerly anticipates an applause for his amazing feats, but instead is met with snide and standoffish responses, often typical of young children. Liam is perplexed and offended by the aloofness of his peers. Naturally inclined to perseverate over such illogical comebacks, Liam would usually react with hurt or hostility and aim to pester his audience into the applause he was expecting. This behavior, of course, would only exacerbate the situation and ultimately botch the play date. In this story, however, Liam recognizes his friends' behavior as snitty and not a reflection of his greatness. He learns to simply accept the rebuffs and move forward, free from the need of his friends' approval.

This is Liam.

Liam is a very talented boy.
He can do lots of neat things, like tricks,
tumbles, and freaky faces.

One day Liam decided to impress his friend Sarah with a super-duper somersault on the couch.

Liam thought he did an amazing job.
Sarah said...

"So."

"Hey Trevor, watch this," said Liam as he performed his most daring scooter stunt. It was the one-legged, one-handed, foot-over-the-handlebar trick. Trevor said...

"That's easy."

"This will gross out anyone," thought Liam, as he pushed his nose to his face, showing the boogery inside of his nostrils.

"Anyway, that's not even funny," said
Ella calmly, quietly, and definitely not even
slightly grossed out.

Liam does not like it when friends don't notice his greatness. They are supposed to say "wow," or "great job," or laugh at your joke. They should say, "That's awesome," even if they don't think so. That is the polite thing to do.

Liam was disappointed and confused by his friends' responses. He felt dumb and not very impressive at all.

Sometimes kids (and adults) do not say what we expect and we can feel annoyed or "let down." Sometimes people just act **snitty** and being **snitty** is not particularly nice.

When kids are **snitty** to you, it does not mean
they don't like you, or that your tricks are
boring. Kids act **snitty** because they have not
yet learned how to be gracious or polite.
They do not know how to behave
like a prince or princess.

When kids act **snitty**, there is not much you can do, other than maybe shrug your shoulders and say, "Whatever." Just ignore them and know inside that you **are** wonderful.

One day at school, Liam wrote a whole page in his journal without help. All his classmates said, "Wow Liam, you are an **amazing** writer!" They were REALLY impressed.

Liam got the award for the "best writer" in his class. He was given a white card with gold writing that was signed by the principal. It said, "Highest Achievement in Writing." "What is so great about this?" thought Liam, as he said...

...a polite "thank-you".

Good work, Liam!